For city sunrises and country sunsets

Henry Holt and Company, *Publishers since 1866*
Henry Holt® is a registered trademark of Macmillan Publishing Group, LLC.
175 Fifth Avenue, New York, NY 10010
mackids.com

Library of Congress Cataloging-in-Publication Data is available.
ISBN 978-1-62779-640-8

Our books may be purchased in bulk for promotional, educational, or business use.
Please contact your local bookseller or the Macmillan Corporate and Premium Sales Department
at (800) 221-7945 ext. 5442 or by e-mail at MacmillanSpecialMarkets@macmillan.com.

First edition—2017
The artist used pencil on paper and digital color in Adobe Photoshop to create the illustrations for this book.
Printed in China by RR Donnelley Asia Printing Solutions Ltd., Dongguan City, Guangdong Province

1 3 5 7 9 10 8 6 4 2

Little Elliot

FALL

FRIENDS

Mike Curato

GODWIN BOOKS

Henry Holt and Company · New York

*L*ittle Elliot and his best friend, Mouse, loved living in the big city.

But sometimes the city was *too dirty . . .*

PHI
QUALITY

BEEP!
BEEP!

too loud . . .

dddrrrrr
dddrrrrr
dddrrrrr

and *too busy.*

"We need a vacation!" said Mouse.

Later that morning, Elliot
and Mouse boarded a bus
bound for the country.

They could see the bright autumn leaves as
the big city slowly disappeared behind them.

Elliot and Mouse got off the bus
and smelled the fresh air.

"Wow," said Elliot. "The country
is even bigger than the city!"

"I'll race you up that hill!" said Mouse.

At the top of the hill, Elliot and
Mouse could feel the breeze and
the sunshine and the soft grass.

Neither spoke for a long time. Then Elliot's
stomach growled. "I am getting hungry," he said.

"Looks like there are some apple trees
down there," said Mouse.

"The country is delicious!" said Elliot.

"And fun!" said Mouse. "Let's play hide-and-seek."

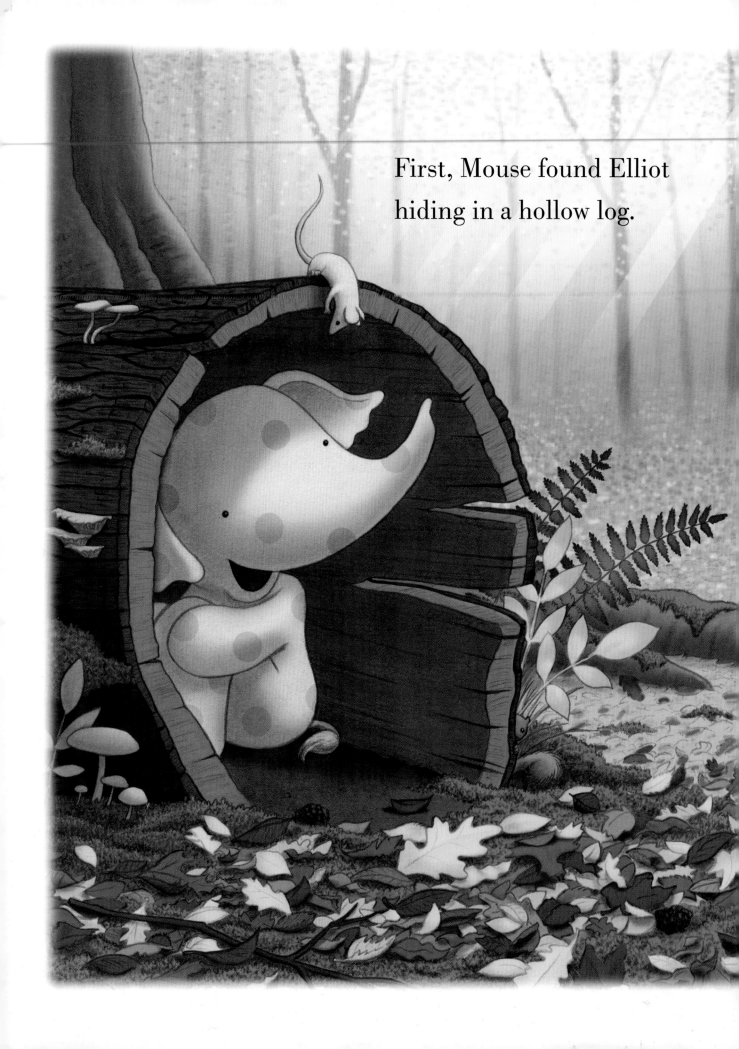

First, Mouse found Elliot
hiding in a hollow log.

Then Elliot found Mouse
hiding in a pumpkin patch.

Elliot picked the perfect hiding place.
Mouse will never find me here! he thought.

Elliot was right.
He waited and waited,
but Mouse never came.

Where could Mouse be?
Elliot thought.

Everything
was still.

Very still.

Suddenly, Elliot smelled something delicious.

Something that smells so good must be worth looking for, he thought.

"I found you!" said Mouse,
leaping from behind the pie.

"Mouse!" said Elliot.

"When I couldn't find
you, my new friends and
I baked a pie," said Mouse.
"I told them you would follow your nose!"

"Nobody knows me better," said Elliot.

Later they all gathered
for a fall feast.

"To new friends!" said Mouse.

"And to new treats!" said Elliot.

That night, Elliot and Mouse nestled
into the hay and took turns naming
the stars until both fell fast asleep.